T0381432

The Big Purple Cat Goes Fishing

ELIZABETH HAMILTON

AuthorHouse™ UK
1663 Liberty Drive
Bloomington, IN 47403 USA
www.authorhouse.co.uk
Phone: 0800.197.4150

Published by AuthorHouse 03/23/2019

ISBN: 978-1-7283-8655-3 (sc)
ISBN: 978-1-7283-8654-6 (e)

Print information available on the last page.

Any people depicted in stock imagery provided by Getty Images are models,
and such images are being used for illustrative purposes only.
Certain stock imagery © Getty Images.

This book is printed on acid-free paper.

authorHOUSE®

The Big Purple Cat Goes Fishing

by Elizabeth Hamilton

Once upon a time far away in the country lived a big purple cat. He used to live with an old lady in a very old house. But when the old lady went to France on a big boat to visit her sister, he had to find a new home.

And that winter, after he walked for miles in the snow, he found a lovely home with Miranda and George and their Mum and Dad. The purple cat had a very nice home now and he seemed to have settled down, since he joined his new family at their farm in the country.

That is, except for the time he ran off on an adventure on his own, but it all went wrong and he was glad to settle down at the farm for the next few months, taking it easy and having fun with Miranda and George and all the family, also teasing the hens who did not like the Big Purple Cat at all. "That cat is too spoiled", they'd whisper to one another. "He is too proud and haughty; he always has to have the best food, with his sausages and cream every day! Miranda and George should give him plain corn and oats just like we have to eat! See how he would like that! But, Miranda cannot see any faults in him! And George is just the same" said the other hen, as they chatted at the side of the house. "But, they'll be sorry, just you wait and see; they'll be sorry for taking that cat in", they muttered as they clucked about the yard.

The Purple Cat lay on his back in his basket twiddling his paws. "Hmm hmmm...it's been very boring around here lately. How long is it since my last adventure? Quite a few months now", he thought to himself, as he dropped the ball of pink wool with which he had been playing back into his basket. "Hmmm, what was that — George calling him again? "What is it now", he wondered and gave a big, boring yawn. "Purple cat, purple cat, my dad is taking us fishing for the weekend! And, as cats don't like water, we thought you'd much rather stay here with Mum and mind the farm with her." He patted Purple Cat on the head.

Then, some time later they waved goodbye to the Purple Cat, as they closed the gate behind them and said they would be back Monday morning, with lots of fresh fish for him to eat. They had left out all his toys and lots of treats for him and thought he would be very happy while they were away.

Purple Cat peered through the red wood farm gate, as they all went out of sight, down the lane. "What do you think of that"? he thought to himself. "They all went fishing and they leave me here with all those boring animals, especially those clucking hens, with no-one to have fun with and throw my ball of wool for me!"

"No way, I'm not having this; I'm out of here!" he said. (I think that was his favourite saying) "If they can go fishing, so can I!" He puffed as he jumped out of his basket. He sneaked around the back of the big, red shed at the side of the farmhouse, opened the old, wooden door quietly and went in to where all the camping gear was kept. He rooted around there for a while and found a torch, a frying pan, a cooking stove and a very, small tent that George used to own when he was little.

The Purple Cat packed them all into the old haversack and tied a polka dot scarf around his neck. He took two packs of sausages out of the fridge and a big bottle of milk.

He crept down to the river at the back of the farmyard where a small boat was tied up with old rope. He then threw the haversack into the boat and jumped in. He untied the rope and pushed the boat far off from the side of the bank and headed off up river.

After a long time in the boat Purple Cat got tired of the scenery and stood up and looked around for a nice place to make his camp. There was a nice, grassy spot just below a weeping willow tree. "That looks nice", he said. "I'm really hungry now. I'll camp here and get the sausages into the pan". He whistled and sang a little tune, as he set up his tent and camping stove.

"I'm the Purple Cat rap rap and this is where I'm at rap rap. I'm very smart at that rap rap, 'cause I'm the Purple Cat, rap rap". "La la la la la la la la la la rap rap La La La La La, 'cause I'm the Purple Cat rap rap."

He rolled around on the long grass laughing out loud at himself."This is cool, I'm so clever; those noisy hens who are always telling tales on me did not see me come out of the farm yard, for once", he said out loud. But they had seen him and nodding to one another they said, "there he goes again; he's up to no good this time." And they shook their heads in disapproval. "He'll be sorry one of these days — he'll go too far."

"What would he do now?" he thought. For entertainment Purple Cat scratched his head. "I know!" He jumped up and started to collect firewood from the bushes. In no time at all he was sitting at a lovely fire. He knew what he needed: some music. He cleaned the frying pan, got two sticks from the ground, turned the pan upside down and started playing his favourite music. He played and played while enjoying the smell of the crackling twigs on the fire and all the night sounds around him. He was having such a good time; music, the fire, the stars overhead and the beautiful smell of the country night air. "What more could he want?" B Bop bop bop B Boom Boom boom born born bom bang bang bang. He was so busy playing his music and banging on the pan, that he did not notice a very large bull looking over the gate of the field behind him. "What are you making all that noise for?" the bull bellowed at the Purple Cat. "I can make noise if I wan't to and banged the pan louder with the sticks."If you don't stop that noise now, I will break down this gate and throw you into the river", roared the bull. "This is my field and my river bank. Now, go asleep and be gone in the morning when I wake up", he roared at the Purple Cat.

Purple Cat went into his tent after he carefully put the fire out. He left his torch on until he was falling asleep, but he could not resist giving one last very, loud bang on the pan. Just before he nodded off, he chuckled to himself as he heard the bull let out another mighty roar. The ground shook under Purple Cat and the big bull stomped on his hooves behind the gate. And Purple Cat thought it was best to go asleep now! "I'll get my own back on that bull tomorrow", he thought."He would not even let me enjoy my great music, which I wrote myself!" He purred and then went fast asleep, very happy indeed!

The next morning Purple Cat woke early. It was a very misty and quiet morning. Purple Cat sprang up on to the gate, where the bull lived. He looked all around; he could see the bull at the other end of the field. Cat took his polka dot scarf from around his neck and waved it at the bull. The bull trotted slowly down the field and started to move faster as he came nearer to Purple Cat, his head down and scraping the ground with his hooves. And then he charged! Purple Cat waved the scarf with his paw and each time the bull came nearer, Purple Cat skipped and danced out of his way, just missing the bull's horns several times. The bull was now very, very angry!

He chased Purple Cat around the field, but his eyesight was not very good and each time Purple Cat escaped. Just barely, mind you — he had quite a few near misses and when he had enough fun being chased by the **bull,** he jumped up onto the branches of the trees overhead and shouted down "you can't catch me now!" as he picked his way across the branches. The bull tried to reach him, but each time Purple Cat would climb higher into the trees. At last he got tired of all the excitement of the bull chasing him and skipped back across the gate of the field.

Purple Cat laughed and got the stove and pan to cook his breakfast. He was having a great time. He cooked the sausages on the stove; they sizzled and jumped in the pan until they were all crispy and cooked deliciously. "Oh! The smell of those sausages in the countryside on your own stove is wonderful", he said as he put them on his tin plate and began to eat the remaining sausages and drank the last of the milk. He burped and patted his tummy. "That was delicious — I need a nice rest now and I'll fish as soon as I wake up", he thought. He put his head back and lay on the lovely, warm grass and fell fast asleep.

Some time later he woke up and realised it was getting quite dark. Better start fishing now or it will be too dark to see. He then got a stick and tied some twine around it and put a fish hook on the end of the twine and sat on the bank. He put the fishing rod into the river and sat there for a long time, but he did not catch any fish; the fish swam by bobbing their heads up and down in the water, looking at Purple Cat. "What a silly cat", they said. "He'll never be a fisher cat." And they swam home to their own little houses under the river. "This is not working" said Cat and left the rod on the riverbank in disgust. He marched back to his tent. Purple Cat got into his tent quite hungry and slept very badly in the cold, misty night, dreaming of charging bulls.

Next morning, looking into the haversack, he realised he had nothing left to eat. He was quite hungry and thirsty now. He went off to the edge of the riverbank and drank some water; then he sat down on the grass and thought "where am I going to get some food — I'm starving!" So then he set off across the fields. There was no sign of the bull now. "He's probably gone off somewhere with the farmer" said Purple Cat. He walked a very, very long way, until he came to a small house, where an old man and woman were sitting outside in the sun. "Do you have anything nice to eat for me? I am out camping far away and have run out of food" said Purple Cat. "We don't give food away" said the old man.

But, if you want to earn some money, there is a whole field of raspberries that need to be picked over there", pointing to a small field at the side of the house. "You pick those and we'll pay you today" said the old man. Purple Cat was not too pleased with this news. He was not used to working at all and this was really beneath him, he thought, but he was very hungry so he did not have much of a choice. He went into the field, collecting the baskets at the gate and started to pick raspberries off the bushes. He worked all day until the sun went down.

When he got back to the house the old woman brought him inside and gave him some milk and a bone. "What does she think I am — a dog'?" I'm not a dog!" said Purple Cat to himself I'm a cat — she's very silly, he said as he shook his head.

"Here's your money", said the old man, after Purple Cat licked the bone and drank the milk. He really was very hungry now. "Buy yourself some nice food and have some raspberries to eat on the way to your camp; goodbye". He put the raspberries in a bag for Cat and off Cat went.

Purple Cat was glad to be going back to his camp; he did not trust that bull and that gate was not as strong as it had seemed when he had seen it for the first time. He hurried back along the country roads. He saw a little cafe painted blue and white and a sign outside saying 'fish and chips for sale'.

He went inside and marched up to the counter, skipping the people in the queue. "How much would it cost for two big fish and a bowl of chips?" he asked the owner who had black curly hair and moustache and was wearing a big, white hat on his head. The Cafe owner's name was Mario. "Look at him, very strange", thought Mario "a talking, Purple Cat!" He scratched his head and counted the money that Purple Cat had put on the counter. "You have enough money for two big fish, a bowl of chips and a fizzy drink", said Mario. "Give me your bag and I will put them in it for you." He wrapped the two fish in greaseproof paper and put them all in the bag for the cat to carry. "I give you the biggest fishes in the cafe; it is the best fish in the world — CIAO!" he said as he waved goodbye to the purple cat. Purple Cat dismissed the people who were glaring at him in the queue for not taking his turn. "What are they all looking at? Don't they know I'm the Big Purple Cat? I hope they did not think I should queue like everyone else!" said Big Purple Cat to himself as he crossed two more fields and skipped through the country lanes.

At last in the distance he could see the riverbank and his campsite. He relit his fire with some more dry twigs, heated his paws and sat back and had the loveliest meal he had in a long time.

He laid out one fish on his plate beside his bowl of chips and his fizzy drink and his bag of raspberries that the old man had given him and ate them **all**. "Where's my frying pan and sticks", he said, looking around. It was not long until he started playing his music again. Bang, bang, bang, bang, rap rap. Rap rap. Rap.

Cat heard a noise behind him; it was the Bull. "Stop making all that racket", said the bull. And push off back to where you came from". "Make me!" said Purple Cat, making faces at the bull and waving his scarf at him. "This is too much", said the bull and with one big run at the gate and a very loud roar, he knocked the gate flat out and trampled across it and chased the purple cat down to the riverbank. Purple Cat just had time to put the fire out with some water he had.

He grabbed his haversack, pan and stove and threw them into the boat as fast as he could. Then he jumped in himself, but he could not get his tent, which that stupid bull had trampled on. "How do you like that?" said Purple Cat angry. "You big bully"! The **bull** snorted at the water's edge. "Don't come back here again" said the **bull.** Cat pushed the boat down the riverbank as quickly as he could.

When Purple Cat got a safe distance away from the bull he grabbed an overhanging branch on an apple tree that was growing on the bank and stopped the boat. "What a silly twit that bull is", he said to the trees. Cat was very annoyed; he fixed his cushion under his head and lay in the boat and ate lots of apples from the tree above, until his stomach started to pain him, from eating so many! The stars twinkled above in the dark, night sky, but now Cat was completely miserable! He turned on his side and rocked himself to sleep in the boat and dreamt of Angry Bulls. When he woke the next morning, he stretched uncomfortably. "That was a miserable night's sleep I had", he said out loud "and all because of that horrible bull".

He washed his face and paws, tied his scarf around his neck and turned the boat around and headed back along the river. He saw the bull in the distance standing at the river's edge. The bull had not spotted Purple Cat — yet!

Purple Cat got out his frying pan. As he stood up in the boat he broke a big stick from a branch overhead and gave the frying pan such a bang that the startled bull jumped nearly two feet off the ground!! He got such a fright he almost fell into the river head first! BANG! BANG! BANG! went the cat with his pan. He glided past the bull in his boat. "You should not be giving cats such frights, as cats can give frights too! ! !" He shouted at the bull. Purple Cat was now laughing so much he nearly toppled over into the water and the last thing he saw of that horrible bull was the bull slipping and sliding up the muddy river bank and almost falling several times back into the water.

Purple Cat's boat now drifted along and it was evening time before he reached the farm. He was so glad to be going home. All of the family were waiting for him at the farmhouse' door, then George and Miranda ran down to meet him."Where were you?" they said, hugging him. "I was fishing" he replied. "And so you were" said George, as he noticed the fishing rod over Cat's shoulder and the fish on the end of the rod. "You are such a great fishing cat. We will not go fishing without you again", said. Miranda, as they skipped up the lane together, She was so glad that they were all back with one another again. "We did not catch any fish", said George, "so we will have your fish for supper tonight" said George as he hugged Purple Cat.

But when they all sat down for supper that night, everyone wondered how the fish was covered in lovely, crispy, golden batter, just like out of an Italian chip shop" But Purple Cat just sat on his high chair, smiling knowingly. "Hmmm, humans don't have to know everything about a cat's life, do they? "No, they don't", he thought to himself.

But that night in the hen house the hens were having their doubts about Purple Cat. "I'd say it's a very tall tale he's telling now", said one of the hens **to** another. She nodded her head in agreement — he has everyone believing he caught a big fish. Personally I think it's just a load of old bull.

The End

Printed in the United States
By Bookmasters